Ten little-known facts about

es

Douglas Little Illustrated by David Francis and Donna Rawlins

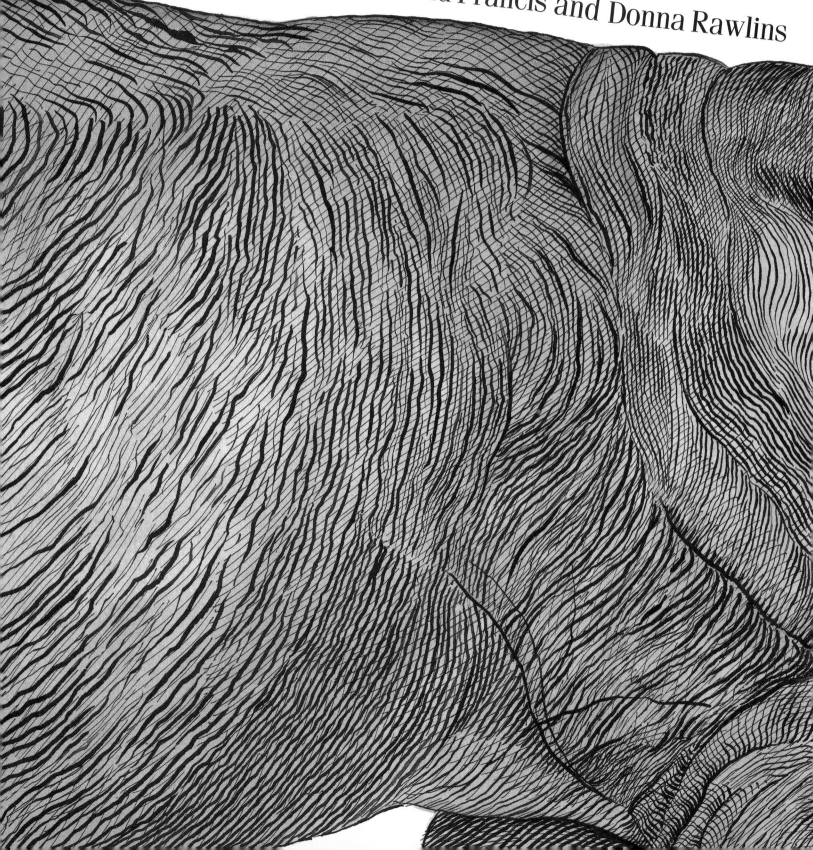

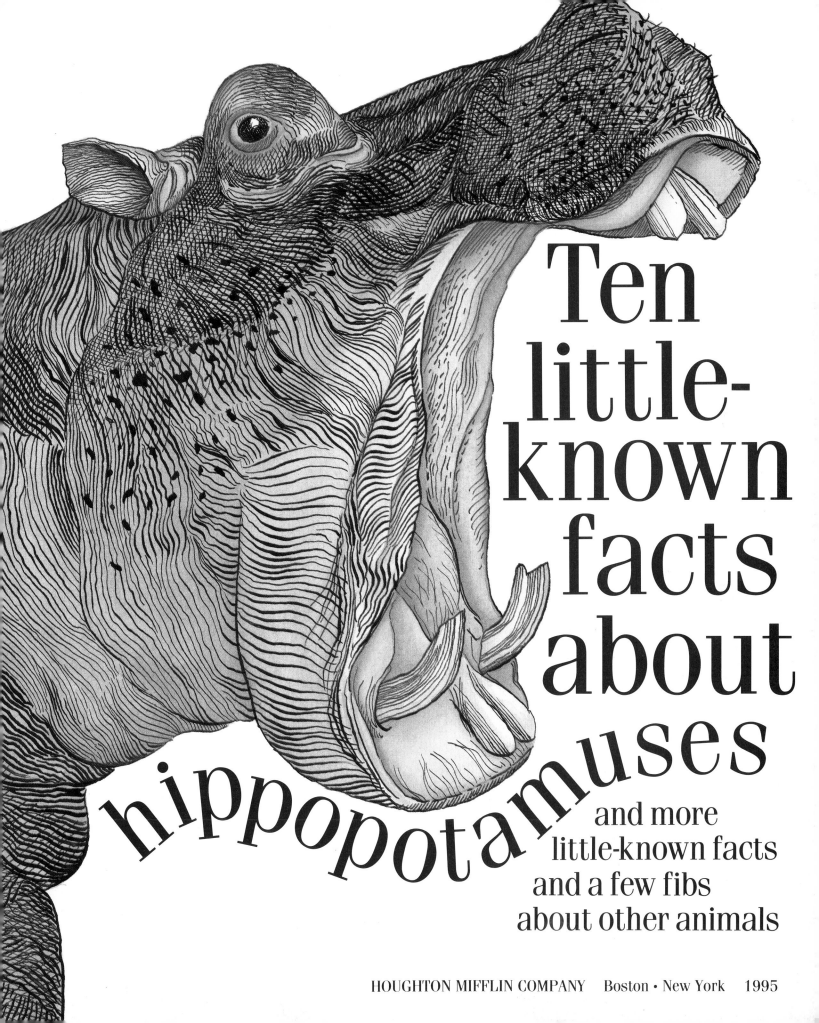

Ten little-known facts about hippopotamuses

and more
little-known facts
and a few fibs
about other animals

HOUGHTON MIFFLIN COMPANY   Boston · New York   1995

For the three muskrat deers, Donna Rawlins,
David Francis, and Chris Cheng, without whose
encouragement, patience, and enthusiasm this
book would not have been possible.

—DL

For Jennifer McAdam, Universal Aunt.
—DF and DR

The author and illustrators wish to thank
Christopher Cheng of Taronga Zoo, Sydney,
Australia, for his invaluable assistance with the
facts in this book. We made up the fibs ourselves.

Text copyright © 1994 by Douglas Little.

Illustrations copyright © 1994 by David Francis and Donna Rawlins.

First American edition 1995 by Houghton Mifflin Company.

First published in Australia by Ashton Scholastic Pty Limited in 1994.

Manufactured in Singapore

The text of this book is set in Fenice and 14-point Caslon Five Forty Roman.

The illustrations were drawn by David Francis with pen and ink,
and colored by Donna Rawlins with watercolors.

10 9 8 7 6 5 4 3 2 1

Library of Congress Cataloging-in-Publication Data

Little, Douglas

Ten little-known facts about hippopotamuses/by
Douglas Little; illustrated by David Francis and
Donna Rawlins—1st American ed.

p. cm.

ISBN 0-395-73975-6

1. Animals—Miscellaneous—Juvenile literature. [1.
Animals—Miscellanea.] I. Francis, David, ill. II.
Rawlins, Donna, ill. III. Title. IV. Title: Ten little-
known facts about hippopotamuses.

QL49.L758   1995

591—dc20   95-1926 CIP AC

Contents

Ten little-known facts about hippopotamuses 6

Sh🍍ppers' guide 10 po ∧

Grrrrrrrreetings 12

Readers' questions 14

The MIX-UP mystery 18

Know your elephant 22

When Isabella spoke bird 26

Tracks 28

Girl meets boy 🌸 Boy meets girl 30

Imaginary creatures 34

Z is for zucchini 38

Sleep 42

Animal classifieds 44

Glossary 46

Ten little-known facts

Everyone knows that hippopotamuses are pachydermatous mammals that are found in the tropical regions of Africa. And it's common knowledge that hippopotamuses delight in water, in living in lakes and rivers, and in grazing on grass and vegetation.

But did you know that . . . ?

hoppabodamzz

It is not easy to say "hippopotamus" with your mouth full.

A hippopotamus can spend all day in the water doing nothing in particular, with only her nose and eyes above the surface, and she can do this without the aid of a Walkman.

about hippo̸tamuses

A hippopotamus can do some things we would love to do. Can you imagine how much fun it would be to walk underwater? A hippopotamus can do this, and when he surfaces for air, after five minutes or so, he expels his breath through his nostrils, making a spout of vapor in the same way that a whale does.

A hippopotamus's head feels so heavy out of water, that if one comes to visit, you should not mind if she rests her chin on your table.

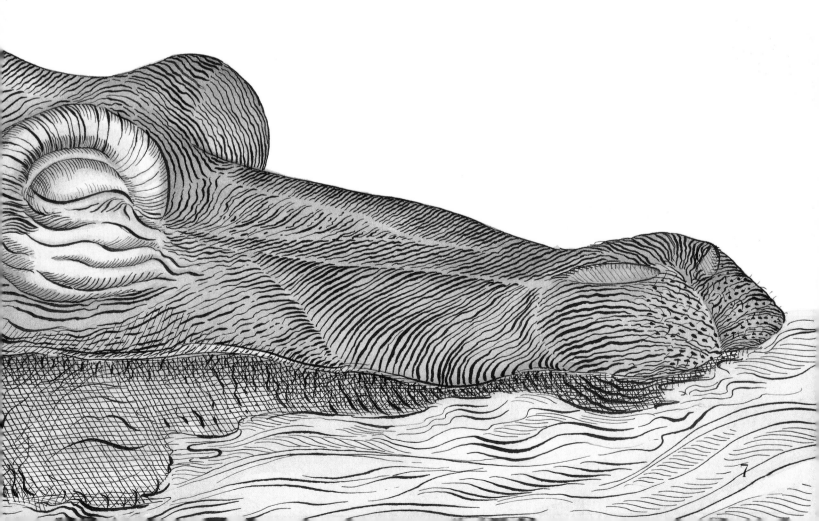

7

A hippopotamus is very large, and of all the land animals only the elephant is heavier. So, when you encounter one at an intersection, remember that the hippopotamus *always* has the right of way.

You must always avoid using sharp words around a hippopotamus. Her skin is so thick that your words will bounce right back and skewer you.

There are two species of hippopotamus. One is the common enormous, round water-loving *Hippopotamus amphibius* (HA). The other is the diminutive forest-dwelling *Choeropsis liberiensis* (CL).

There are HA HA HAs everywhere in tropical Africa. They are party animals. But there are very, very few CLs left in the wild, and they are excruciatingly shy.

The name hippopotamus comes from the Greek words *hippos* ("horse") and *potamus* ("river"), hence a "river horse." Now if *hippos* is a land horse, and hippopotamus is a river horse, and *hippocampus* a sea horse (*kampos* means "sea monster" in Greek), then what would a *hippoaero* look like?

A hippopotamus lives in a large group of anything from 10 to 150 or so. You'll need to be careful when you invite one home to lunch. Don't say, "And bring the 'family' with you."

A hippopotamus has a huge mouth which he can open very wide. What a pity he is a vegetarian. He has the perfect mouth for a hamburger.

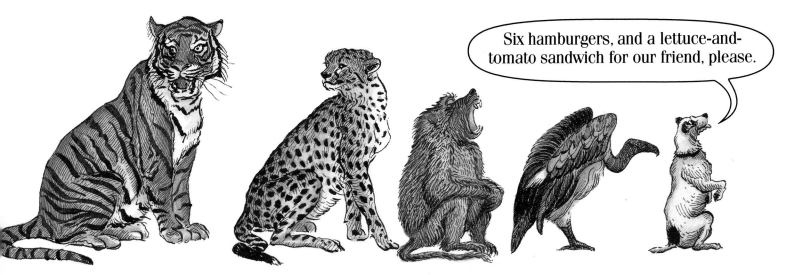

Six hamburgers, and a lettuce-and-tomato sandwich for our friend, please.

Shoppers' guide

You will often see people coming out of the greengrocer's with loads of fruit and vegetables and a hapless echidna (spiny anteater) jumbled in with the cauliflower and lettuce.

When these shoppers arrive home, they exclaim, "Where is the pineapple?" and are so embarrassed when they realize their mistake.

Here are ten easy ways to help avoid this confusion:

There is a difference in coloration. The pineapple has a tendency to range from green at its top, through yellow, to orange at its base. The echidna ranges from mottled beige at the top and sides, to a muddy brown around the legs and feet.

There is a difference in movement patterns. The pineapple tends to move in one direction only—upward—whereas the echidna can move upward, downward, and forward.

There is a different attitude to offspring. A mother echidna will carry her young in her pouch, usually for about three months until it becomes unbearably prickly. (If you want to know how this feels, just put a pineapple down your sweater.) The baby echidna then accompanies her mother for another nine months before setting off on her own. Pineapples, on the other hand, reproduce by budding a new plant. This new plant grows up to become its parent's next-door neighbor.

They differ in their social groupings. Pineapples lead regimented lives in groups of 1,000 or more. Echidnas live the life of Gypsies, wandering by themselves, following the food trail.

They differ in their food-gathering techniques. Echidnas have long sticky tongues with which they gather their food, such as ants and termites. Pineapples have roots to draw up nutrients from the ground, and smooth green leaves filled with chlorophyll with which they gather sunlight.

They differ in ripeness tests. To tell if a pineapple is ripe, you tug at one of the leaves that grows out of its crown. If the leaf comes out easily, the pineapple is ready to eat. If you tugged at an echidna's spines, it would squeak and roll itself into a ball. This means that the echidna is not ripe, and shouldn't be eaten.

They differ in their responses to danger. Echidnas will quickly dig into the ground and bristle their spines if you say "BOO!" Pineapples show no visible response to scary noises.

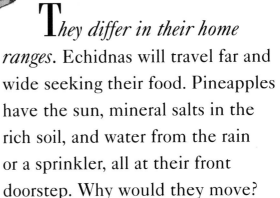

They differ in their home ranges. Echidnas will travel far and wide seeking their food. Pineapples have the sun, mineral salts in the rich soil, and water from the rain or a sprinkler, all at their front doorstep. Why would they move?

They differ in their reliability. A pineapple will always stay where you put it—patiently waiting. But an echidna will wander off, almost involuntarily, from where you put it down.

They differ in their characters. Pineapples are sweet and juicy. Echidnas are more complicated.

Grrrrrrr

It is no use trying to shake hands with a horse. But, if you know one well enough, you might rub her nose and say, "Whoa there, girl" in a neighborly kind of way.

You *almost* could shake hands with an elephant. Elephants use their trunks to greet each other. So, you could hold out your hand (if you had a friend who was an elephant) and he would probably shake it with his trunk.

You *could* shake hands with a cat, but it wouldn't mean anything to the cat. Felines greet you by flicking their tails up. But they do like to hear you say, "Hello, cat" just the same.

reetings

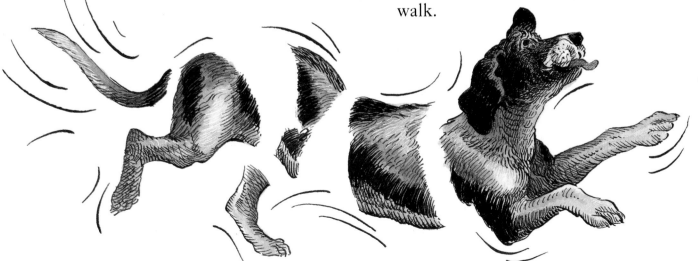

Lizards would *not* shake your hand. They would flick out their tongues and taste the air and smell your distinctive odor. That is about as far as a lizard will go, *vis-à-vis* social interaction.

A very friendly dog would probably shake hands, or at least put his paw on your face at five in the morning. Then he would shake his rear end until his tail fell off, then his back legs, then his middle, which is a complete nuisance since it forces you to get up, bolt all the parts together again, and take him out for a walk.

Could you shake hands with a spider monkey? Spider monkeys have the most elegantly long fingers, but although they are equipped to shake, they would probably greet you with a shriek.

Q Readers' questions

One of the most frequent questions I am asked is, "How can I attract birds into my backyard?"

It is not hard to attract many species of bird if you are prepared to reshape, replant, and restock your outdoor spaces.

Kookaburras are some of the easiest birds to cater for. Simply scatter small snakes and lizards over the grass and laugh loudly. They will soon want to join the party.

Seagulls, being scavengers, are likely to respond to a mountain of household garbage liberally sprinkled with fish heads. A less-smelly alternative is to arrange rows of park benches in your yard and hold gala garden parties where you serve fish and chips wrapped up in old newspapers. The seagulls will provide the entertainment.

Loons, *cormorants*, and other swimmers and divers. Excavate a large hole at least 150 feet deep and construct a saltwater pool. Stock with fish. Install several underwater observatories with glass windows. Watch out for frigate birds and skuas in the airspace above the pool, for they will try to steal the fish out of the beaks of the fish catchers.

Flamingos are always a treat. Make a shallow lake with a muddy bottom. Stock this lake with brine shrimp and load your camera.

Cockatoos are not picky eaters. They are the bird equivalent of a herd of elephants (who sometimes push over trees and eat the branches). A sure-fire winner with the cockatoo is to clear your backyard and sow it with wheat. When the ears are ripe, the cockatoos will appear. Oddly enough, cockatoos like to eat wood, so plant a very large tree in the middle of the yard and build a small wooden house next to it. The cockatoos will eat the house.

15

Swifts, *swallows*, and other insect eaters are best observed at night. This is not because they are nocturnal—they are not—but it is easier to control the insects after dark. Release bogong moths (several thousand per hour) into the air. Hold their attention with searchlights probing the sky. Then hope that some of the insect eaters are still awake and hungry.

Emperor *penguins* need a fair amount of commitment. Freeze a large part of your backyard to a depth of 6 feet. Add an icecap that's at least 3 feet deep. Construct a saltwater pool stocked with fish, seals, and krill. Air-condition the entire space to –68°F. Then put on your top hat, tails, and gloves and wait for the penguins' inevitable arrival.

Suburban *songsters* may present less of a challenge. Sometimes these birds are already in your yard but you might overlook them because you like to sleep until it is too late to hear their dawn chorus.

Don't despair. Try installing a lighting system that will simulate sunrise in your bedroom. Make sure it automatically switches on two hours before the real sunrise.

But there will be no need to spring out of bed. You'll still have two whole hours to rest before the songsters begin.

Hummingbirds and *honeyeaters* are attracted to flowers, so arrange an assortment of vases throughout the yard and fill them with flowers of the season.

Roadrunners. Remove all good soil and replace it with gravel and sand. Plant sparsely with thorny scrub. Heat the air to 91°F. Add a coyote and some peccaries for atmosphere. Stock with small lizards and desert rodents. Make sure all obstacles are cleared away to allow the roadrunners to run laps around the yard at high speed. They like to exercise.

If you like *ox peckers*, construct a large pool of fresh-flowing water surrounded by grassland. Half-fill the pool with hippopotamuses, and stock grassland with elephants, wildebeests, and zebras. The ox peckers will suddenly appear, as if from nowhere.

Hopeless causes. There are several birds that just cannot be accommodated in backyards.

The *albatross*, with a wingspan of 11½ feet, soars on the breeze over thousands of miles without thinking of landing.

Vultures have disgusting eating habits (the less said about them, the better).

No matter how dedicated you are, it is just too late for the *giant auk*, the *moa*, and the *dodo*.

Dung birds are definitely out.

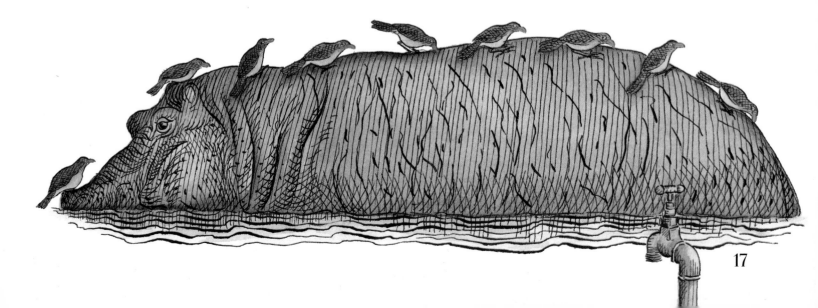

The Mix·up mystery

Many people have thought long and hard about why animals look the way they do. Why do they have such unlikely coverings? Some have smooth skins, some have fur, some have shells, and some have scales.

Hundreds and hundreds of books have been written about this baffling question.

May I tell you of my experience when, as a young naturalist many years ago, I saw something that may solve, once and for all, this most puzzling conundrum?

It is a little-known fact that, like cabinetmakers, bus drivers, and milliners, animals used to have an annual picnic.

And it was at one of these picnics that the fur really started to fly.

The picnic had been progressing smoothly. The peccary had his snout in the trough. The elephant and the giraffe were competing to see who could reach higher (the elephant, by standing on

his back feet and stretching his trunk, was ahead). The lion was lazing around the barbecue area. The tortoise and antelope were racing in the 100-meter dash and the 400-meter slalom. The boa constrictor was winning the slow race.

The sloth and koala were both napping in the sun. The emu and ostrich were trying to cross the language barrier by using sign language.

Of course, many of the animals were making pigs of themselves, and some were outrageously and unashamedly boisterous.

But when the temperature reached 104°F, most activity slowed to a trot. Then someone suggested they all go for a swim.

Well, one thing led to another, and before you could say "Last one in is a rotten egg," they had all taken off their clothes and jumped into the river, skinny-dipping in the cool currents.

There on the bank lay fur coats, feather ensembles, hairy overalls, scaly skivvies, abandoned shells, suits of armor, slippery wetsuits, woolen sweaters, and countless body suits in various shades.

They were all carefully placed and neatly folded.

Well, they were until the toucan and the spider monkey (the South American duo who had earlier performed an aerial samba through the treetops) began to quietly rearrange the outer garments of the swimmers. Feather was changed for scale. Fur for shell. Hair for armor, and so on.

What a mess when all the animals emerged, dripping and laughing from the water! The ostrich could find only a feather coat. "Where are my scales?" she cried.

The elephant found a thick, heavy hairless skin. "Where's my striped fur coat?" I heard him bellow.

The tortoise couldn't find a thing to wear, so she crawled into a shell. "Where is my lovely stripy skin?" she sobbed.

The llama could find only a long-haired rug. "Where are my beautiful feathers?" he lamented. The lizard, who emerged last out of the water, was left with a slippery wetsuit. "Where is my ginger fur coat?" I distinctly heard her hiss.

They were all terribly embarrassed. Who *were* these creatures they were seeing, whose shapes were so familiar, but who looked so very, very odd?

They shambled around, red-faced, for a while, and then quietly drifted off to the four corners of the world, to adjust to their new clothes and to puzzle earnest scholars through the ages to the present day.

Know your

Everyone knows that elephants are pachydermatous mammals, like hippopotamuses. And *everyone* knows that the African elephant (*Loxodonta africana*) is larger than the less-common Asiatic elephant (*Elephas maximus*). And it's common knowledge that they walk about twice the normal human walking pace and feed primarily on a diet of leaves and grasses.

But did you know that . . . ?

One study showed that 44 percent of the food elephants swallow is not digested, and passes through their bodies unchanged.

This probably explains why, although elephants are very fond of wild fruits, I have yet to see one elephant on a pineapple plantation.

There are some similarities between people's teeth and elephants' teeth. Both have incisors, or cutting teeth, in the front. And both have molars, or grinding teeth, in the back.

But the elephants' incisors protrude and are called tusks, while we human beings are tuskless.

Elephants have only 4 molars, whereas we have 12 all together.

An elephant's molars do so much hard work that they wear out and have to be replaced five times during her lifetime. By the time elephants are fully grown, their sixth set of molars are bigger than bricks.

Imagine crunching on a stick of celery with four bricks in your mouth.

elephant

Elephants have a way of speaking to each other that is completely inaudible to human beings. They can speak subsonically, making sounds that are too low in frequency for our ears to detect.

Hence the fact that you never see elephants ejected from the movies for talking, or even sent outside the classroom for whispering in class.

If you are relaxing, stretched out on the grass, and an elephant plants his foot right near your head, you may be curious to know whether he is an African elephant or an Asiatic elephant.

According to *some* books I have read, you could simply count his toenails.

The African elephant, they say, has four toenails on his front feet and three on his back; the Asiatic elephant has five toenails in the front and four in the back.

Therefore, if you counted four toenails, you would either be in the fortunate position of just having been passed by an Asiatic elephant, or the unfortunate position of being about to be passed by an African elephant.

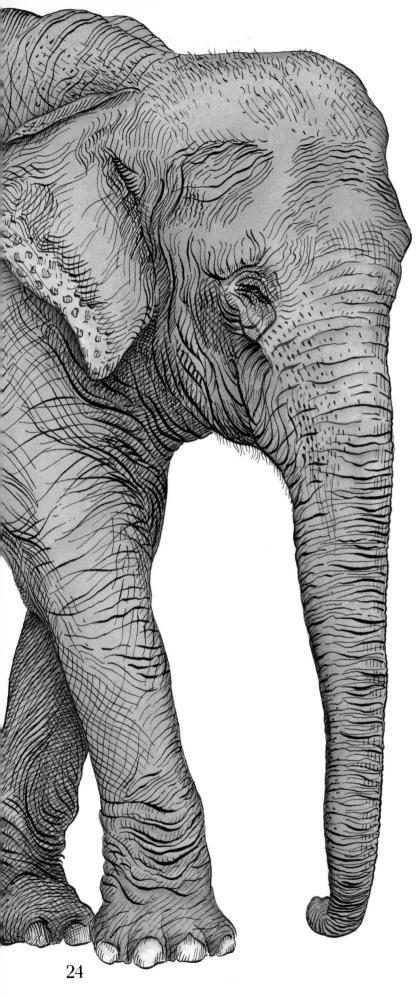

POSITION VACANT: Would you like to be a zoological statistician? This position calls for an enthusiastic young person who would be willing to travel widely.

Background information: Although elephants' feet look as uncomplicated as tree trunks, they are in reality as complex as a crossword puzzle.

Inside their feet, all elephants have enough toe bones to make five toes on each foot, but on the outside they choose to grow toenails on only some of these.

Since the books referred to on the previous page were written, other elephant experts have discovered that African elephants can have four or five toenails on their front feet; and three, four, or five on their back feet. And Asiatic elephants can have five toenails on their front feet and four or five on their back feet. But nobody knows exactly how many there are of the various combinations.

Job description: The successful applicant will count all the toenails of all the elephants in the world. The applicant should have a sunny disposition, should be able to mingle freely with elephants, live on a vegetarian diet, and count to five.

If an elephant just happens to come by after you have poured some fresh concrete—and if this elephant steps in the wet concrete, and if then he engages you in a lengthy friendly debate—you might find it awkward to raise the topic of the concrete.

Don't worry. Part of his feet are made of soft spongy material that broadens when he puts his foot down on the ground, and then shrinks again when he lifts it.

So, just say good-bye when it's convenient, and although the concrete may have set, he will stroll off without even noticing his *faux pas*. You can use the neat round holes to plant some shrubs—perhaps elephant ears.

Elephants have an acute sense of smell. They can detect people upwind of them half a mile away. If you had an equal capacity, you could smell half the dinners cooking in the neighborhood and your brother would have to stow his sneakers either downwind or in the next town instead of under his bed.

An elephant's skin looks like a wrinkled baggy suit that is several sizes too large for him or her. If the elephant took off this suit to send it to the cleaners, he or she would look like this.

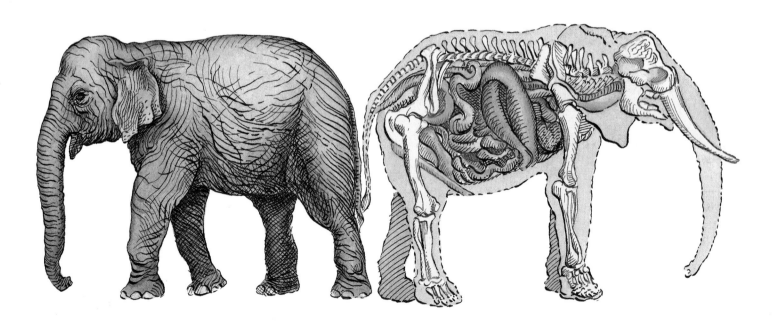

When Isabella spoke bird

Animals certainly talk to each other, but their talk varies more than ours. They shout, they squeak, they click, they growl, they sing, and they even commune in languages too high-pitched or deep for our human ears to hear.

In short, they communicate differently from us.

Just how differently can be seen in the experience of 12-year-old Isabella who, by some misfortune or magic, found herself unable to speak human language but perfectly able to speak Bird.

When she awoke on that fateful day she found herself perched on the end of her bed, twittering.

What's happening to me? she meant to say, but as she opened her mouth she sang a little song instead. Fortunately, this

singing session stopped quite abruptly when the sun streamed into her room. So she dressed and hopped into the kitchen. Inexplicably, she felt a constant hunger (for she had birdish feelings as well) and she pecked away at her cereal until she had emptied the box.

Her brother, Buzz, sauntered in and, completely overlooking the fact that Isabella was perched on the edge of her chair, twittering, spoke excitedly about a movie he had seen the night before.

He hasn't listened to a twitter I've said, thought Isabella. I wonder if he ever does?

Rowdy, Isabella's cat, walked in. Isabella felt very uneasy, and hopped onto the table.

"Wow waa, wow waaa," said Rowdy. Strangely, Isabella could still understand Cat, for she knew that he was saying, "Come on, come on, feed me." So she quickly hopped down and fed him, taking particular care not to open her b . . . mouth. She was taking no chances.

The dogs next door began to bark, "Urf arf, urf arf." But Isabella couldn't understand their language and flitted off to catch the school bus.

On the bus she saw her boyfriend, Conway (though he didn't know he was her boyfriend). Almost involuntarily she started to sing. She twittered a little, trilled a little, then warbled some. Conway hid behind a seat.

Isabella, undaunted, continued to fill the bus with her courtship song. (How embarrassing!)

School was even stranger than usual. Isabella didn't like being cooped up, and although she knew the answers to many of the teacher's questions, she could respond only to the ones for which a nod or a shake of the head was enough.

Soon after recess, two lorikeets started feasting on the blossoms just outside the window, near where Isabella was sitting. She hardly noticed them until she heard one say, "Human education is a bit far-fetched, isn't it, Birdy?"

"Yes, Lori, and the singing! They do drone on and on, don't you think?"

Isabella bit her wooden ruler to stop herself from twittering uncontrollably.

"Pay attention! Pay attention, Isabella!" said the teacher.

Isabella glanced out of the window occasionally during the afternoon, but the lorikeets were gone. At last, the school day ended, and she boarded the bus home.

For some strange reason, Conway was nowhere to be seen. So Isabella, without knowing why, didn't sing.

She darted from the bus stop, dumped her school bag, and perched on the windowsill. Other birds flew by and, remembering the lorikeets, Isabella listened carefully, trying to catch what they were saying. Some had accents too thick for her to understand, but not the sparrows, so she called out to them.

They asked her what had happened to her feathers, and why she spoke so loudly, and what she was doing inside the house. Fortunately for Isabella, she couldn't get a twitter in edgewise, for she had no answers to any of their questions.

Then they asked her to join the choir for the Going-Down-of-the-Sun Ceremony.

She agreed and as the sun set, all the birds twittered madly. Slowly, one by one, they stopped and fell asleep, as did Isabella, with her head tucked under her arm.

Next morning, when the other birds were singing the Brand-New-Day Ceremony, Isabella opened her mouth and said, "Hooray." And, not surprisingly, she spoke Human nonstop all day.

Conway sat behind her on the bus and said, "Do you want to come over to my place and see my talking parakeet?"

Isabella twittered, blushed, put her hand over her mouth, and nodded.

However, if neutrinos are not massless, but have a small mass of their own . . .

Tracks

Paleontologists can tell much about dinosaurs from the shape and depth of their tracks. Some dinosaurs are known to us only by their footprints.

It is said that if you measure the outline of an elephant's footprint and multiply it by 3, you will have the elephant's height. (This may be just coincidence, but when I measured the circumference of my own footprint, 40 inches, and multiplied it by 3, it was exactly my height!)

Examine the following tracks closely. What do you make of them? Who or what made them?

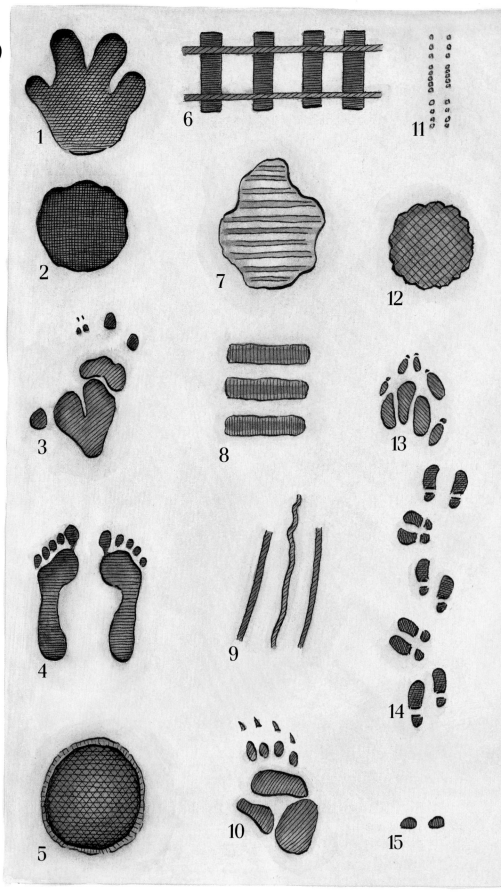

28

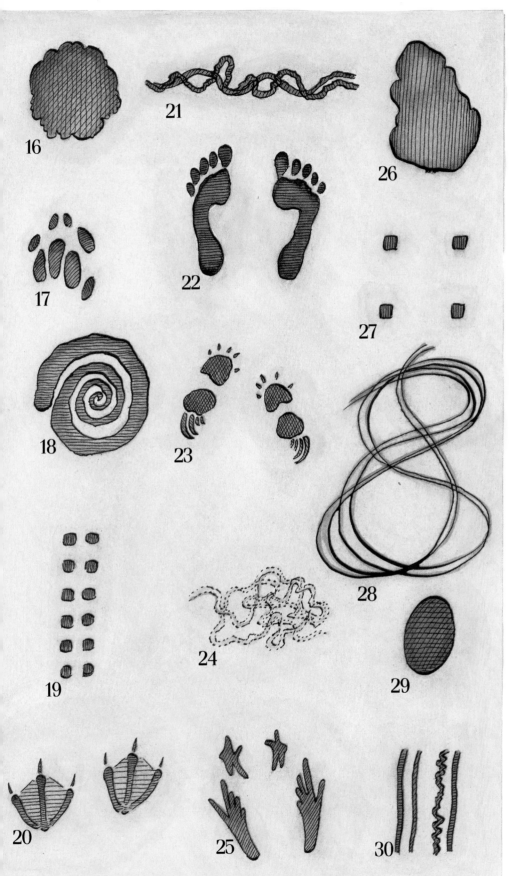

Key

30 Supermarket cart
29 Teddy bear
28 Ice skater
27 Chair
26 Chocolate frog
25 Frog
24 Ants
23 Echidna
22 Woman
21 Bicycle carrying 14 circus performers
20 Seagull
19 Egg carton
18 Orange peel
17 Four gherkins, three jellybeans, and one peanut
16 Cauliflower
15 Ballet dancer
14 Mail carrier
13 Thylacine
12 Pineapple
11 Caterpillar
10 Wombat
9 Tricycle
8 Three spring rolls
7 Ridged potato chip
6 Railroad track
5 Meteor
4 Man
3 Koala
2 Elephant
1 Hippopotamus

Girl meets boy

Some of the simplest things in life can become the most complicated. Take romance, for example. What could seem more simple? Boy meets girl, girl likes what she sees, romance blossoms. How could you possibly make such a simple event complicated?

Well, here are some actual examples of the ways things can go wrong.

Boy meets girl, girl likes what she sees but is unable to make any sound come out of her mouth. A different girl meets a different boy, he likes what he sees, stumbles, falls over, and hides under a very flat rock. Now you are saying, "That's silly. It will never happen to me." And maybe you are right. But just in case, I have prepared a guide to romantic behavior, compiled from the courtship rituals of birds. (It may be quite a while before you need to use this advice, so keep this book somewhere safe, like under your pillow, so you will know where it is when the time comes.)

30

Boy meets girl

The male tern (boy), when courting a female tern (girl), catches a small fish and presents it to her. *This is a good idea. Give a gift.*

Now when the female (girl) accepts the fish, the male (boy) cunningly doesn't let go, and thus a tug-of-war ensues. *This sometimes works and sometimes doesn't.* It is called teasing. Not everyone likes it.

The male lyrebird (boy), in order to attract a mate (girl), fans out his magnificent tail. *This is another good idea: extravagant display.*

Consider the case of a certain Clark Kent. He wore horn-rimmed glasses, a conservative hat and suit—and loved Lois Lane. But Lois couldn't see him. To her he was invisible. So Clark decided to try *extravagant display* just like the lyrebird.

He put on a blue body suit. He wore his red underpants on the outside. And he completed his outfit with a red cape and boots, and his initial boldly displayed on his chest.

This worked wonders. Lois fell for him in a big way. (But it wouldn't work today. Every gym is filled with hundreds of women and men dressed like this, and no one notices at all.)

31

The male bowerbird (boy) makes an arched space with branches and leaves. He then decorates this space with sparkling objects, often of the same color. He might collect bits of blue plastic, a blue clothespin, blue glass . . . He then waits outside for a female bowerbird (girl) to come along and be attracted to his taste in interior decoration.

This is an exquisite idea.

But don't take it too literally. Remember, the objects the bowerbird collects are completely ordinary. It is the *blueness* he collects. It is a mistake to litter your bower with skateboards, sweat-shirts, and chocolate bars, when what works best is completely free. A sense of fun is a good place to start.

Female (girl) flamingos and male (boy) flamingos engage in formation dancing, gracefully bobbing their slender necks as they wheel back and forth in the shallow water. *This is a great idea.* Several hundred rubber-booted couples dancing in formation in a shallow lake soon produce giggles, chuckles, and spasms of laughter. And if you can laugh, who cares about talking?

The majority of male birds (boys) attract their mates (girls) by the simple technique of singing. If a female (girl) of the same species likes what she hears, she will join in the song. If you find yourself alone, walking down the street, scrambling through thick undergrowth in a steamy jungle, sailing single-handedly across an ocean—just sing and see if anyone joins in.

The male ostrich (boy), who is flightless like all ostriches, tries to impress the female ostrich (girl) by beating his gorgeous wings and looking as if he is going to fly.

This is a fabulous idea.
No matter how you feel on the inside, look good on the outside.

The female ostrich (girl) doesn't mind that the male ostrich (boy) doesn't actually take off. It is enough that he looks as if he really could fly if he wanted to.

Postscript

Girl meets boy. She likes what she sees and gives him a fish. Boy puts on his brightest red cape and then pretends to fly. She takes him to a disco, wearing rubber boots. He decorates his room with pictures of dinosaurs. She's outgrown dinosaurs and leaves, singing. It's all quite simple!

Imaginary

I love to hear stories
about imaginary creatures—
fantastic creations like dragons
and mermaids.
I know they could never have existed,
but sometimes, when I look around,
I blink hard and say,
"Isn't that a . . . ?" And then,
"No, it couldn't be!"

34

creatures

Take the talking tree. Legend has it that, during one of his campaigns, Alexander the Great came upon a talking tree. This tree told him that no good would come of his desire to conquer more and more lands. Moreover, he could find himself cut off far from home.

A fifteenth-century miniature painting depicts this tree as having branches that end in different kinds of heads. I suppose that when those heads weren't giving good advice to passing kings they would just chat among themselves.

What is there, I asked myself, in everyday life that has trunk lines and branch lines that end in talking heads?

You've guessed it: the telephone system. And many a person has received helpful advice over the telephone just before being cut off, a long way from home.

Or what about the two-headed snake? In classical myths, this creature has a head at both ends of its body. It is known as the *amphisbaena*, which means "goes both ways."

I was thinking about them last Saturday, while fishing on the pier. I looked up and, lo and behold, there was one approaching me: a harbor ferry.

Now a harbor ferry has two identical ends, like an *amphisbaena*. When it reaches its destination, the skipper just walks to the other end and the stern becomes the bow, and all is ready for another voyage. Of course, it would be more like an *amphisbaena* if there always were two skippers, one at each end, and one end of the ferry could talk to the other end just as an *amphisbaena* could— if an *amphisbaena* could talk, that is.

Or, consider the shape-changers (or *baldanders* as they were called), who are described in the seventeenth-century novel *Adventuresome Simplicissimus*.

The hero, Simo, is wandering through a garden. He touches a statue, which is really a *baldanders*, for it instantly changes into an oak tree, then a sow, then a fat sausage, then a field of clover, then a pile of dung, then a flower, and so on. You see how sneaky they are!

Well, I was sitting in my room wondering about them, late on Saturday night, when I saw something that began to change at frequent intervals without any warning whatsoever.

This looks uncannily like a *baldanders*, I thought. And as I watched closely, it changed again into a stagecoach lurching across the saltbush plains. Then it changed into a bowl of soup, then into a bottle of shampoo, then a vacation island, then a fast car, then a sofa (on sale)— and then back into a stagecoach again.

Progress has enabled us to buy a list that will tell us some of the things the modern *baldanders* will change into. It is called a *TV Guide*.

Z

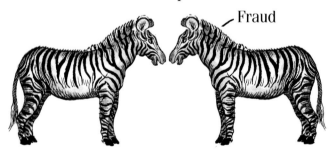Everyone knows that zebras are odd-toed ungulates, cousins of the horse and ass, who live in Africa and eat mainly grass.

But did you know that . . . ?

All zebras have stripes, but no two zebras have the same pattern.

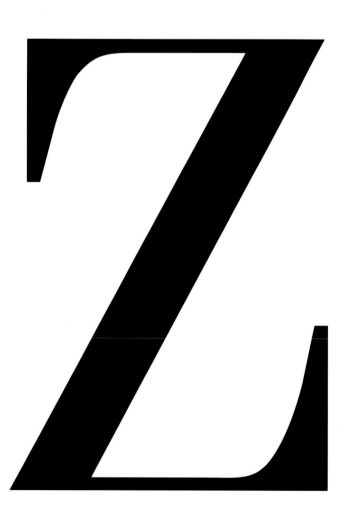

Fraud

This is not the case for manufactured things; so, if you find yourself with two identical zebras, one of them is a forgery.

All horses in the Northern Hemisphere have their birthdays on January 1. And all horses in the Southern Hemisphere have *their* birthdays on August 1. But zebras think that any time they return from drinking at the water hole without being eaten by a lion or a pack of hyenas is their birthday.

Zebras invented the idea of the rear-view mirror. While grazing, they often stand in pairs facing in opposite directions. In this way they can avoid colliding with an oncoming predator.

As well as inventing the rear-view mirror, zebras have shown themselves to be experts at encoding systems.

When a zebra foal is born, its mother maneuvers herself so that the first thing the baby sees is her unique markings. They look something like this . . .

ISBN 0-86896-621-

9 780868 966212

The foal then scans this pattern and imprints it on its memory. It is always able to decode this zebra message from the hundreds of similar ones that crowd around it. Naturalists call it the Ma code.

is for zucchini

Zebras, like mules, are very stubborn. You know, of course, that before color television, everything was black and white and gray. And when color television came, it transformed the world.

Well, zebras defiantly refused to change. So today, along with killer whales, magpies, pandas, and penguins, zebras remain the last relics on earth of that bygone era known to videologists as the B&W Period.

Zebras are sociable animals. They never wander around or play by themselves, but always prefer company. Studies of human beings have shown that, unlike boys, young girls don't usually play by themselves, but most often form small groups. Hence the famous old saying: *Zebra? Girl? Zebra? Girl? If it wasn't for their braids, you couldn't tell them apart.*

Zebras come in three sizes: small, smallish, and medium. The smallest, standing 12 hands high, are the mountain zebras from southern Africa. The next, standing 13½ hands high, are the plains zebras from a little farther north in central Africa. And the largest, standing 15 hands high, are the Grevy's zebras of northern Africa.

Imagine what would happen if zebras spread to the northern- and southernmost parts of the globe. They would range in height from the Greenland zebra, the size of an elephant, to the Chilean zebra, the size of a piglet.

Without zebras, alphabet books would have pictures of zucchinis on their last pages.

Z is for Zzebra

Sleep

At school, sleep was one of my favorite subjects. In Kindergarten Miss Kestrel would spread mats on the floor so we could practice sleeping.

But in the next year, the new teacher (Mr. Spry) seemed totally unaware that there was even a subject called Sleep.

So all further studies of this topic had to be conducted on our own.

We formed a secret club called Research Essential to Sleep Technique, REST, and with our official club names we undertook studies in special departments.

We all considered this amazing fact.

"You mean they went to sleep before I was born and still haven't woken up?"

"Yes, and if one were to go into a torpor today," said Dozy, "when it awoke we would be finishing high school."

Blinking Bazz specialized in the sleep of horses and cows who, impressively, can sleep standing up. Bazz tried it (unsuccessfully) at home but woke on impact with the floor. Then he *almost* succeeded one really hot day on the way home from baseball practice in a jam-packed bus. He traveled probably a couple of stops before his knees buckled.

As he was slipping downward he awoke, and just before he disappeared from view he saw through the tangled mess of bodies a classmate on crutches

z z Z Z Z Z Z Z Z z Z Z Z Z

Those of us who were interested would trade information on the subject.

"Did you know," said Sleepy Sue, "that cats and dogs dream?"

"No," we said.

"Well, they do."

"And did you know," said Dozy Dougal, "that some insects can stay in a torpor [Dougal's favorite word] for more than ten years?"

with both legs in plaster.

As he hit the floor he exclaimed, "That's it!"

This was later confirmed by Miss Willow (the nature studies teacher) when she said that horses and cows are able to lock their knees when they sleep. "Also," Miss Willow said, "birds can lock their claws around branches—and bats and one type of parrot can sleep hanging upside down."

Blinking was challenged by this last revelation.

Noddy Nelson was fascinated by hibernation and the animals who can sleep through the whole winter.

While she suspected her teenage brother was close to perfecting it, she knew *she'd* never get away with it. By the third week someone would definitely miss her at Brownies.

So, instead, she aimed at the longest daily sleep records held by the koala and the sloth, who can sleep between 17 and 20 hours a day.

Noddy made it to 14 hours after staying up all night talking to Somnolent Sally.

Somnolent was more interested in short, quick sleeps. In fact, she found that there were some creatures, such as sharks and swifts, who could actually sleep while they continued to swim or fly.

Somnolent tried to keep talking while she dropped off to sleep, but her words became slurry and eventually stopped.

Miss Willow told her that the sharks' and swifts' kind of light sleep was really more like daydreaming. Now, daydreaming was Somnolent's greatest talent. All she had to do was to stop talking and empty her thoughts, and she could pass a whole class in the company of the sharks and swifts (and go wherever it is that daydreamers go).

Nap-Nap Norton announced one day that parrotfish can surround themselves at night with a mucous sleeping bag which prevents their enemies from smelling their scent. When it is daylight, they eat their sleeping bags and swim away.

There was a hushed silence in REST as the members imagined eating their own sleeping bags, made of kapok or feathers. Nap-Nap decided against it.

"Predators," explained Miss Willow one hot and lazy afternoon, "doze after they have eaten. And the length of time they spend dozing depends on the size of their meal. The most amazing of them all is the python, who can swallow a gazelle whole! Then the python spends up to six months in a torpor, digesting it."

After this wonderful story, which could only have come from a real enthusiast, Miss Willow was made an official member of REST and given the name Weary.

To celebrate, she took us all out to a huge lunch.

FORMAL
POOL PARTY?

Call Penguinwear for
a personal fitting.

Strictly classical
black-and-white
evening wear for
that glamorous
end-of-year function
by the pool.
The best quality
fabrics, soft as down,
so comfortable for dancing
(and swimming).

AMUSEMENT SYSTEMS

THRILL
SEEKERS!

Is your life a little humdrum?
Does nothing ever happen?
Are you bored?

We'll come to your house, school, or office
and scare the living daylights out of you.

Call Mobile Howler Monkeys!
(Discounts for senior citizens)

PETS,
SMALL

No backyard?
Apartment dweller?

Are you forbidden the
joys of pet ownership?

Call now for your almost
invisible pet.

**Click Beetle, Nematode,
and Silverfish, Inc.**

44

TIRED OF ALWAYS BEING LAST IN LINE?

For a small weekly fee, rent our company name and put your business ahead of the rest!

AAAAAAARDVARK

Aaask for Aaaanthony or Aaaaalicia.

SQUASH CLUBS

If you enjoy a competitive game of squash, but can't find the right partner, look no further!

Phone now for a free consultation.

CALL JUNGLE GYM

(Speak to B. Constrictor)

PARTY LIGHTS

No more messy extension cords to trip over.
No smelly flares to sting your eyes and attract moths.

Call
Fireflies
Party Lights.

Available in one pulsating color.

Squads of 500.

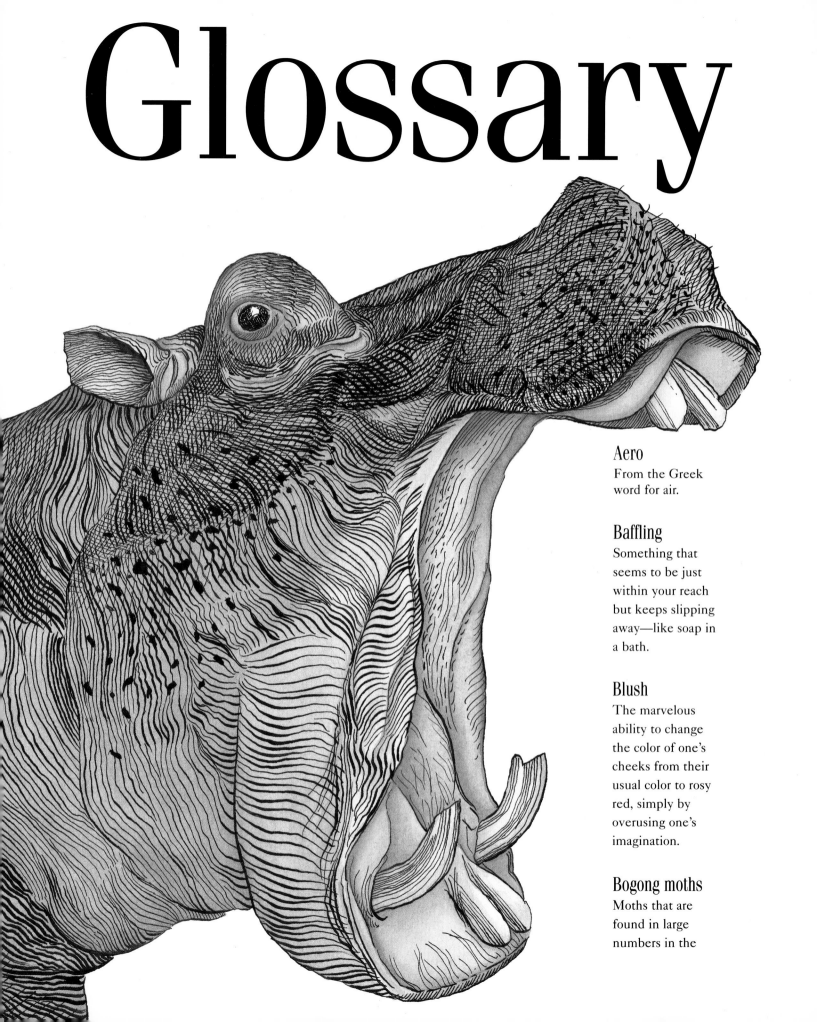

Glossary

Aero
From the Greek word for air.

Baffling
Something that seems to be just within your reach but keeps slipping away—like soap in a bath.

Blush
The marvelous ability to change the color of one's cheeks from their usual color to rosy red, simply by overusing one's imagination.

Bogong moths
Moths that are found in large numbers in the

coastal lowlands of eastern Australia. During the warmer months they migrate to the Australian Alps where they then estivate (see *hibernation*) in rock crevices all summer. Zillions of bogong moths were blown off course by the wind and invaded Sydney in January 1988.

Brine shrimp

An extremely small shrimp that lives in very salty lakes.

Cabinetmaker

An expert who makes wooden cupboards, wardrobes, drawers, and bookshelves that do not fall apart when assembled.

Chlorophyll

The green substance in plants. It traps the energy from sunlight, which helps plants absorb the carbon dioxide and water they need to live and grow.

Conundrum

A fancy word for riddle.

Courtship

Attracting to yourself a boyfriend or girlfriend, so that they may remember your name (and telephone number) and hold you in their thoughts. Sometimes leads to matrimony.

Daydream

To rest with your eyes open—hence the expression, "the lights are on, but nobody is at home."

Diminutive

Less than large, less than middling—small.

Echidna or Spiny anteater (pronounced *ih-KID-nuh*)

A spine-covered, insect-eating, egg-laying mammal of the monotreme family, found in Australia and New Guinea.

Fact

Usually something that is true.

Family

People who compete for the bathroom every morning.

Faux pas

A social blunder. The literal translation from the French is "false step."

Feline

Belonging to the cat family. A feline, however, will not pound on the bathroom door and ask if you've finished in the shower.

Forgery

A copy pretending to be the original. Some forgeries are easier to detect than others. For example, it is unlikely that the picture of the *Mona Lisa* on the cookie box in your kitchen is the original. The real *Mona Lisa* does not have "Family Assortment" written across her forehead.

Grazing

Eating living plants for breakfast, lunch, and dinner.

Greengrocer

A storekeeper who sells mostly fruit and vegetables, but who may also sell nuts, juices, soft drinks, honey, and cans of whole tomatoes and tuna fish. Not to be confused with a grocer who has an excess of chlorophyll.

Hands

Horses, donkeys, and zebras kept stretching their necks when people tried to measure how tall they were, so everyone agreed to measure their height to the top of their shoulders. And, because horses are such ancient companions of people, and have been tamed for at least 3,000 years, they were measured in hand widths (rather than with the modern tape measure). So, a horse is described as "standing 15 hands high." A hand is 4 inches. So a horse 15 hands high would be 5 feet at its shoulder.

Hibernation

Literally means "passing the winter." *Estivation* means "passing the summer." They both refer to the ability of some animals to close down certain body systems and slow down others so that they can pass a whole season in a deep sleep.

Hunger

This is the empty feeling people have in their stomachs that forces them to return, time and time again, to the supermarket. It usually occurs only a few times a day. However, some animals are continuously hungry. A bird, for example, can spend up to 20 hours a day eating, and can consume up to twice its own body weight in food every day.

Inaudible

Unable to be heard; sometimes because the sound is too high or too low, and beyond what the human ear can detect. On other occasions, a sound may be said to be inaudible when the maker of the sound is confronted with a challenging question. For example, "Where is your homework, Eugene?" Eugene's mumbled response will probably result in the teacher's saying, "I'm sorry, Eugene, but your reply was inaudible."

Kapok
A fiber, similar to cotton, that grows on a tropical tree and is still, in some places, used to stuff mattresses, pillows, and sleeping bags.

Krill
Tiny shrimp-like creatures. Not so different from brine shrimp, except krill live in freezing-cold oceans, and brine shrimp live in hot salty lakes. Krill are eaten by baleen whales, and brine shrimp by flamingos.

Mammals
Animals who love their mammies.

Mermaids
The female counterparts of mermen. A species that can live at the beach, but can never wear a pair of thongs.

Milliners
Hats, hats, hats. That's all they ever think about.

Nocturnal
Active at night. Animals who say "Good night" when they wake up, and "Good morning" when they go to sleep.

Odd-toed ungulates
Imagine all the animals who have hoofs. Now, which of these have one or any other odd number of "toes" on each foot? Do horses? Do tapirs? Do rhinoceroses? Well, they are some of the odd-toed ungulates. When you have exhausted this list, try looking for the even-toed ungulates. Which animals have 2, 4, 6, 8, 10, 12, 14, 16, or 18 "toes" on each foot?

Offspring
Children and their animal equivalents: foals, cubs, kittens, pups, piglets, calves, fingerlings, cygnets, chicks, joeys, fledglings, etc.

Pachydermatous
Thick-skinned.

Paleontologist
A scientist who searches for, finds, and studies fossils in order to understand the prehistoric world.

Shriek
Much louder than a scream or a shout. A sharp, shrill cry. One would find a shriek useful in the event of stepping on an echidna or a scattered box of thumbtacks. However, a shriek would probably not be necessary were one to step on a pineapple.

Species
In order to understand the millions of creatures on Earth, scientists have ordered, or classified, them in groups. A species is one of the many categories in this classification system. Generally, a species is a group of plants or animals whose members have details in common, and can interbreed.

Television
One of the many ways people have of talking to each other. When the commercials come on, people talk.

Thylacine (pronounced *THIGH-luh-sign*)
An extinct Australian animal that looked like a wolf, had a striped back like a tiger, and raised its young in a backward-facing pouch. Thylacines, as a species, survived until July 10, 1936.

Torpor
A very deep sleep in which the whole body is slowed down to a fraction of its normal activity, thus allowing animals and insects to use less energy while passing a winter or another long period of time.

Underpants
Also called undies. These are made of soft fabric such as cotton or silk and are the first garments to be put on in the morning, and the last to be taken off at night. They are rarely seen in their natural habitats except on the clothesline.

Vis-à-vis (pronounced *veez-a-vee*)
Literally translated from the French means "face to face." We use it to mean "in comparison with," or "if you consider one thing alongside another." For example, a tortoise is a very fast walker, *vis-à-vis* a rock.

Zucchini
A vegetable, related to the zebra by alliteration.